THERE IS ONLY ONE
GHOST IN THE WORLD

THERE IS ONLY ONE
GHOST IN THE WORLD
Sophie Klahr and Corey Zeller

FC2

TUSCALOOSA

FC2 is an imprint of the University of Alabama Press
Inquiries about reproducing material from this work should be addressed
to the University of Alabama Press

Book Design: Publications Unit, Department of English, Illinois
    State University; Director: Steve Halle, Production Assistant: Pica
    Williams, Production Intern: Kylie Hagmann
Cover photo: Courtesy of the Klahr Family
Cover design: Matthew Revert
Typeface: Baskerville URW

Library of Congress Cataloging-in-Publication Data is available from
the Library of Congress.
ISBN: 978-1-57366-203-1
E-ISBN: 978-1-57366-905-4

This book is dedicated, humbly, to our families.

>>>>

My mother was reading a book to me in bed when we saw the reflection of flames on my bedroom wall. Across the street, the neighbor's house was burning. I remember being outside in my nightgown, barefoot, my feet in the runoff the firetruck bled, ambulance-men rustling onto the stretcher something dark. My parents told me later that our neighbor, the old woman I called Aunt Heppy, had died, and that her old white dog had died too, but that her German shepherd puppy had survived. It jumped through the big glass window of the living room, breaking the broad pane. At school, everything was uniform. The kids all wore the same outfits and their parents all had the same medications. You looked out the window most of the time. You learned more than anyone should ever know about the sky. You drew a line with a stick in the new snow and dared a friend on the other side to cross it. *Once you cross it, you can never come back,* you told him. He was reduced to tears, and you got in trouble, even though his explanation made no sense to anyone. *They told me I could never come back,* he wailed. Only when I was grown-up did I realize that it couldn't be true, that the puppy could not have broken the glass. I asked my mother, and she admitted: it wasn't true.

>>>>

There is a kaleidoscope of chemicals Elijah takes now—chest bound, pre-op, new hormones rattling like private thunder, sweet peppering of stubble on his jawline. I am pained when the checkout girl calls him *Ma'am*. We stand drinking Coke in the thick Texas night outside the washateria, giggle at a chain of raccoons running by on their tiptoes. He is studying theology. *God is doing for us what we cannot do for ourselves,* he says. You have a poster on your fridge with an illustrated geologic timescale. There is a nautilus, an armored fish, a stegosaurus, an owl. Eon, era, period, epoch. Earth forms approximately 4.6 billion years ago. In the middle of the night, baby mice fall from the rafters onto the bed, looking like kidney beans glowing in the dark. The mice are too small to have been climbing on their own—their mother was trying to take them somewhere. Four have fallen, and you wonder if the mother managed to save any. If by now she is sleeping in her somewhere, holding at least one of the lives she made. You remember a teacher telling you how water was made in second grade. You memorized the periodic table. All those little boxes: pale blue, pale pink, pale yellow. The kid with leukemia who sat in front of you would pass you the pictures they drew. Stick figure drawing a stick figure. Stick figure drawing a house. You drew your own body and passed it back. One day the kid was a solid. Later a gas. Then he evaporated. *This,* the teacher said, *is how you make a cloud.*

>>>>

Your half sister's mother in Arkansas shoots the old sheep she owns. It has grown very sick, and she doesn't have the money to put it down. Then she shoots the donkey that loved the sheep and that the sheep loved. Your half sister explains how her mother believed keeping the donkey alive wouldn't be fair. She didn't want to leave the donkey like that out in its pasture, always waiting, always looking for the sheep. Or perhaps—and worse—leaving the donkey out in the pasture knowing how deeply alone it was now. Her mother had a neighbor dig a hole, and shot both animals beside it, one after the other. Rolled them into the hole together. Is this what mercy looks like? I can hear it in the deadbeat sky leaking longline, hooked hard; in the gristle of decades crunching like red pills at the heel of my hand. We watch an episode of *Cops*. A dog drifts through the scene outside a trailer. *Good dog,* says one of the cops.

>>>>

Despite legend, the Bermuda Triangle does not have a higher rate of disappearances than other geographical sites. It does not appear on a single world map. At present, Alaska ranks as having the most disappearances per capita. Though California ranks as the state with the most disappearances: 2,133 people. Sri Lanka has the most disappearances in the world: 60,000 to somewhere near 100,000 missing people since 1980. If you look at Sri Lanka on a map you'll see it looks like a human nail. And oddly, yes, like a triangle. Laid out in one long line, the average child's blood vessels would stretch over 60,000 miles. The woman who will become your next lover is describing her divorce while she gives you a lift to the airport. When she begins to talk about taking off the wedding ring, her hand cramps, and she opens the window to press her left hand into the wind. You were engaged once. It was months after the proposal that your fiancé actually gave you a ring. Christmas in Virginia, your first time at his family's home, and he presented the ring to you in front of everyone. It was a family ring, an opal. When you put it on you thought, *My god, he doesn't know me at all.*

>>>>

A child is walking with its imaginary friend in the snow. *Maybe we've lost our awe in nature,* the child says to its imaginary friend, *that's why I want to ask you... a wild animal.... What do you think we're put on earth to do... what's our purpose in life? Why are we here?* The imaginary friend wears a long red scarf wrapped smartly around its neck. The child has on a blue coat, blue mittens. *We're here to devour each other alive,* smiles the imaginary friend.

>>>>

That shadow you were watching earlier freezes in place like an icicle from a gutter. It stays there, still, even in the dark. Once, you were standing near a warehouse with your friend Natalie, both of you looking up at the big icicles you knew better than to stand near. One falls and cuts her cheek. You were jealous of how your mother placed a Band-Aid on Natalie's face, her hand cupping Natalie's chin in a foreign gentleness, and you want to be cut by something, to have someone else's mother touch you. Now you're looking online for a new winter coat to buy, but every one that you like is over five hundred dollars. You like what lines a coat best, not the armor of it. Or perhaps that is the armor: the lining, the seams, where everything starts. The interior pocket at the breast, so when you go to retrieve your house key, your hand passes over your heart. If you had this coat, you'd think of the Pledge of Allegiance each time you reached for your key. It's funny, the places we put our hands when we promise something.

>>>>

Rehab, a few days before Christmas. The inhabitants are sitting around stringing popcorn onto a scarlet thread, or eating the popcorn they are supposed to be stringing onto the thread. A Sandra Bullock movie where she plays an addict is yammering on the wheeled-in television under the uneven fluorescent lights. Everyone is trying not to fall in love with everyone else's wounds. *It's not my first rodeo,* someone says. The Twelve Steps are emblazoned in medieval-looking script on a plastic banner that hangs centered on one wall, making the wall the center of the room. Soon, everyone will pull their folding chairs in a circle. A circle represents an endlessness. As a kid, they told you to "Stop, Drop, and Roll." They told you this is how to smother a fire from your body. Which is a strange verb, isn't it? *Smother.* To cover something doused and blazing. To give it so much it goes out.

>>>>

I book a two-night stay at a motel on a beach at the end of a peninsula. One is required here to book at least two nights. It is the cheapest room: two double beds that open to the water. The last time at this motel, the woman whom I'd invited to come pointed out a constellation of a bear. The story was a violent one: a Greek god once had an affair with a nymph, and in order to protect her and her son from his jealous wife, he turned them into bears. Then threw them into the sky. The woman pointed and I followed the length of her arm. Stood behind her, with my hands on her hipbones, and looked over her shoulder, over the arm that pointed. I pretended to see what she wanted me to.

>>>>

Someone tells you that Brian Wilson wrote "God Only Knows What I'd Be Without You" to impress his father. His father wasn't impressed. Years later, he went to see his childhood home and there was only an overpass, and the shambled dirt all overpasses hold beneath them. The arc of eulogy. You want to put a heron in the eulogy, an egret. A living shape that stills the sky.

>>>>

Whatever it was I wanted from you was an accident, a dilemma. The row of low apartments look like blood on a bandage. In the newspaper, an interview with a man who herds sheep: *Like poetry,* says the man, *whistling does not need to be useful in order to be special or beautiful.* Beautiful things are nice but they owe us nothing. There's a line in a book I like about how spaces can love and hurt one another as if they were solid. Sometimes I end up living my life this way: a hurt space. You looked at a frog frozen in the creek and said that maybe when the ice thaws it will come alive again. It's one of the things I liked best about you: how you said the things a child would, despite knowing better. "Knowing better." That's not the right way to say it.

>>>>

This is the second time you've missed your son's birthday. The year before, your car died. Two guys jumped out of their car and tried to help you. *There is no way to fix this,* one of the men said. You called a tow truck and sat on the hood of your car. You thought of your son sitting at your parents' kitchen table in front of the supermarket birthday cake. You thought of your mother saying, *He really wanted to be here.* "Remorse—is Memory—awake" wrote Emily Dickinson. "Everyday objects shriek aloud," wrote Magritte. By the time he was around fifty years old, Mark Rothko had stopped giving artist's statements. *Silence is so accurate,* he said, and killed himself about fifteen years later. You make a grocery list. Grapefruit, gum, seltzer, cigs. *How are you doing today?* a friend asks.

>>>>

Lou sits in her jeep in New Orleans in the rain, putting on makeup to go to a party with people she barely knows. Purple lipstick. At her catering job, a man solicits her for sex. *It's not that I don't have a price*, she tells him, *it's just that I'm not in the mood.* Her brother is writing a rock opera about a boy whose father breaks his jaw in an irreparable way, and leaves him in the wilderness to fend for himself. He doesn't want the boy to learn about the cruelty of the wider world, and so he does this for the boy, breaks him before he knows how the rest of the world could break him. Breaks him before anyone else has a chance to. For all of one September, I listen to one song on repeat. The girl who sings it is well known for wearing a skeleton costume: a black sweatshirt and black sweatpants with decals of bones printed front and back. There are omissions, expansions. There is how often I used the word "whittled" in my twenties to describe a feeling. A common vacancy, the back of a lover, a glass jar of bees. Jupiter and his 63 moons. Overheard: the older woman across the street, talking to her stocky beagle: *I know, I know. You expected something different.*

>>>>

You have done many bad things, but you are a good person. You meet your father at a baseball field and offer to pay back all the money you owe him—a lot. He declines. Instead, he reads aloud a poem that he wrote when you first went to rehab, a poem which he has never shown to anyone. "Despair Now" the poem is called. When he folds it back into its quiet square and hands it to you, the world seems for a moment to be mended. On TV that night: an antique roadshow, a reenactment. Can we change? That most ancient human argument.

>>>>

Iceland, 2012: "When the details of the missing person were issued, the woman... unwittingly joined the search party for herself. After a night-long operation involving around 50 people, the 'missing woman' eventually realized she was the source of the search and informed police." The police chief later told a newspaper that the woman simply didn't recognize the description of herself, and (quote) had no idea she was missing (end quote). The word of the day is "contronym": a word with two meanings that are each other's reverse. E.g., "cleave" means both "to sever" and "to bind together"; "ravel" means both "to tangle up" and "to disentangle." Also "sanction," "bolt," etcetera. Mosquito flicker, a cold case; a railroad town that long has lost its railroad. Standing at the roadside, I imagine what creatures would have eaten me here—this whole state was underwater once. Lightning coughs on the ridge of pine. I look up and imagine the water. While hunting, one should not forget the wind. Never ever forget the wind while hunting.

>>>>

Everything I learned about gender as a child now makes me ill. The triangle torso of a woman on a restroom door like a caution sign. The false exclamation point invisible inside her. I do not want to be pressed against a pronoun, or to ever press a child against one. I want to be like the jungle frogs who can impregnate themselves, and I want to choose not to.

>>>>

Bunny told me once, walking through a park at dusk, how smoking crystal meth felt: like horses galloping through his veins. That's how he described it: *like horses galloping*. He went to India with a photograph of the guy who gave him HIV, kept the photograph in a freezer for two months, then buried it. I spend an afternoon reading about the electromagnetic fields around our hearts. I grow out of myself the way roots grow over a grave. I wake every day rubbing a seam I found in the stratosphere. Bunny started saying he heard voices in the walls, in the floorboards. He started calling straight people "breeders." He told me that he saw a dead pig in the canal, bloated, where there was no pig. He drove north, to the Russian River. And one day, he simply disappeared. No. Not simply.

>>>>

You have been waiting a year to receive a single unemployment payment. You call and after a dozen tries finally get ahold of a woman. She is silent for a long time on the phone. While you wait, you flip through a glossy book of abandoned malls. Shattered skylights. Dried-out fountains. Plastic vegetation. You listen to her type for a while, before she finally reports back. *Well, it seems I've found the problem,* she says, *it looks like someone forgot you.*

>>>>

Fish have something in them called a lateral line—this is what helps their schools stay together. When they want to stay still, they face upward. Into the current. The day closes itself like an orphan's locket, the lip of a candle resembling lace almost touching the inside of a thigh. Now, and only now, you fail to find a difference. Some handless beauty. Blinking and squinting at the clearest possible scene. Truth reversed does not make a lie. A lie reversed does not make truth. The truth of the person is different than the truth of the poem. You try to make a Venn diagram of this, but can't figure out what to put in the third circle or in the pill shape of the intersection. A certain type of ants collect the skulls of other ants to decorate its nest. There is a type of shark that new theories say may have a lifespan of up to six hundred years. In Greenland, one is caught that scientists estimate as being between two hundred and seventy-two years old and five hundred and twelve years old. There are certain types of crystals in the eyes of this shark. The oldest type of poetry is poetry with a riddle inside.

>>>>

Are you indestructible? you ask your kid. He is playing a video game. *Nope,* says your kid. Your kid starts crying. You have to console him. *Hey, we've been through this before,* you say. *We've still got each other,* you say. He is looking at you with bleary eyes, red-faced. You think of how you'd look at him sometimes at night crying red-faced in his crib when he was a wordless infant. *We just got here,* he says. This is true. Sometimes you think your lives were better when he was wordless.

>>>>

There is the photograph of your older brother, far off, on a single-sail sailboat. You touch the photograph and wish you could have known him then, this boy nicknamed Sloth in high school for his slow lope down the basketball court. There is the photograph of him holding you proudly, in nothing but your yellow Cheerios shirt and underwear. You are both beaming. He is holding you in the same way that in another photograph, he holds his black Labrador, these little armfuls of a life with only enough translatable language to say *I am hungry* or *I am sleepy* or *I am happy and I want to run; run with me.* Your favorite cousin sends you an article. The headline is "Five newborn blue-tongue skinks found under a pile of shoes." She tells you that she's going to release her new music under the title of *Maror*, as in the bitter herbs eaten at the Passover seder. After the shooting at your synagogue, you both felt more Jewish: more small, more clear. When you were young, you cracked her head open while playing a game, you spinning her around by her hands: you let go at the wrong moment and she hit the stairs. She went wild-scream-bleeding through the kitchen where her mother was, and bleeding wild-screaming into the living room while you both ran after her as she flung herself on the couch. *Not on the couch!* screamed her mother.

>>>>

You had a friend in high school who interned at a hospital who stole a bunch of X-rays. You got high and she hung them with tape from strings she hung in her room. A broken arm. A tumor. Someone's ruined heart. Christmas lights illuminating the pieces like constellations that have stories no one quite remembers entirely. It felt wrong looking inside people and now, it seems, everywhere you go someone is looking inside of you. A broken promise. An argued memory. Someone's ruined heart. *I'm a good person*, you tell your friend, standing in the dry yard the next morning. A single gunshot goes off and you both turn your heads toward the noise, but no other shots come. *I know you are*, she says. A girl you loved once loved you more and got angry when you didn't love her like that, like, back enough. She is angry enough to say that you aren't queer enough. This is always the problem—others drawing little boxes around your desire, waiting at a long panel like a spelling bee competition, waiting for you to fumble.

>>>>

I want a lover who will bring me small useless things. A keychain from Roswell. A lollipop with a scorpion in it. A magnet in the shape of a state. It turns out—I can forgive almost anything, so far. I think of words that sound the same but mean different things. Refuse (refuse), Lie (lie), Entrance (entrance). How wind can wind. I have a certain kind of nature. If left alone, and wet, a cloth of kerosene may burst into flame. Sometimes I get a word caught in my mouth, a word like *forsythia* or *vertebrae*. If you listen closely to the lyrics of disco, so many seethe with refusal: *You dance and you shake the hurt,* goes one song. Disco has much to do with pointing as you dance. *THIS* is what I will do, says the pointing. The pointing of a finger extends a body beyond its space. Takes up the air, affirms what is. What's next? All *the love in the world can't be gone,* goes one song, *all the need to be loved can't be wrong.*

>>>>

Your father sends you a book about trees, about how they talk to one another. Now that he's retired, he is writing something like a memoir. He calls what he is writing "Dad's Pointless Stories." His father owned a jewelry store and fixed watches. He was a justice of the peace and almost officiated the wedding of Arthur Miller and Marilyn Monroe, but instead of getting married in Connecticut, they eloped somewhere else. A few years later, Monroe was dead. *And that's how myths are broken,* your father writes, *by reality.* Later, the jewelry store was robbed. Your father's mother and father were made to lay facedown on the floor while a man with a gun looted the store. Your father has told you that he regrets not visiting directly after the incident. How he believes that his mother never quite recovered. This element of the story is not yet in the something-like-a-memoir, and you wonder if he will include it at all. But he hasn't gotten to that part yet.

>>>>

They didn't know what they wanted. Chrysanthemums, tempests, the sacred heart. The next-door neighbors put their grill too close to the fence and the dry vines catch on fire. Across the street, the obese woman is screaming again at her boyfriend as he exits the house. He gets in the driver's seat and she lays her body on the hood of his car. A child watches from their first-floor window. These streets are an anorexic arm—cars park on both sides of the street, two tires on the sidewalk. It gives the neighborhood a tilting sensation, as if the whole city were suspended. This is just how we live. Looking to the outside world as if everything is about to fall. You were very little the first time you decided to run away. It is a story your mother tells you later. You filled your tiny red-and-yellow shopping cart with stuffed animals and went down three houses, to the end of the street, where, your mother tells you, because there was a stop sign, you stopped.

>>>>

Before me, my mother had a baby that died inside her. She had to carry it inside her for months, your best friend says. This is her habit—to sideswipe you with facts. It is amazing how many times you've fit your whole life into a car, a resident of nowhere, a stowaway inside a stowaway. All you need is one mug, one bowl, one fork and knife and spoon; all your silverware is someone else's, picked up from one roommate or another. There is the can opener your mother gave you years ago, one of those times when she filled a brown paper grocery bag with oddities as you left: a scarf, a few pens, a can of pears, baking soda, a magazine with an article she thought you'd like. You were already standing in the front hall with your coat on when she started filling the bag. *Do you have a can opener?* she yelled from the kitchen, *I'm giving you a can opener.* It all sat in the back of your car for months. At some point the bag ripped, most of the contents spread nude across the back seat. You wondered what someone would think if they peeked in. What kind of person is this, they'd wonder, with this lonely can of pears.

>>>>

Janus words are named for the Roman god usually depicted as having two faces, one that looks toward the past and one toward the future. He presided over doors, gates, passages, all beginnings, all endings, all lulls between war and peace; Janus was responsible for time. A Janus word is one that can be used with opposite meanings, for example: *cleave*. For example: *rock* or *fast* or *fix*. You had only a few friends during your first months in theatre school—one was a boy called Janus. He had short dreadlocks and smelled like clean laundry dried from brittle water. Early that first fall, you and him and your big-eyed friend Kate bought ecstasy, then went to watch a live performance of Pink Floyd's *The Wall* in the auditorium of the student center. He kissed one of you, then the other. Years later you will run into Janus in the East Village; he will have his child with him. You will not have spoken for ten years, and when you say his name to catch his attention, he looks shocked. He greets you warmly and says he doesn't go by that name anymore.

>>>>

A friend tells me that I am just a bird in a forest who will delicately and thoroughly regard another bird from a distance, then fly to its side and eat its heart. He tells me this and a cloud moves so quickly through the thin clearing that it startles me. All day yesterday it threatened to rain, storm systems on every horizon. All you really need to do in a storm is be ready for it. Imagine that: a bird that eats another bird's heart.

>>>>

I pray to a listening god, you say. The house is a chrysalis. We listen to the wind hum about it as if the walls are about to split, as if we were one half of a migration. Reason and Desire are both good in a fallen world; once moral judgment is made, understanding stops. Whenever you drive past Juliet Street, you think of the night you spent nearly overdosed there. How someone strong carried you from the car up the stairs. *Don't rape me*, you remember joking, despite the fact that in your life by then, you'd already been raped twice. In the morning it was raining, and you woke to a bunch of other teens strewn around the room, looking like puppies asleep in little piles. You were the first awake. You remember looking outside at the rain and thinking, *Soft rain.*

>>>>

Are they someone I should know? is a phrase you find yourself saying often to others. Meaning, *are they someone who has done something that will change how I move though this world, even if just for a moment?* Optimism is a chandelier. It swings to one side catching some light. It swings back and catches the dark. Pessimism, on the other hand, is nothing but a weathervane, a lightning rod. On the internet, you learn that figs aren't a fruit: they're an inverted flower and depend on death; every fig contains the carcass of a wasp. It should be easy to make poetry of—a tear-shaped bruise that grows from a tree—but you are tired. You leave open the Google search tab on figs, believing something will come of this. Another time. A treeless orchard. Yet all about you, as you brush your teeth, as you go through the apartment turning off lights for the night, the smell of rotting fruit. The sound of it falling.

>>>>

Ricky Ray Rector, a mentally ill man on death row, is served
his last meal. He is going to be executed tonight. He gets a
steak, cherry Kool-Aid, and a piece of pecan pie. He asks one
of the guards to save his pie so he can have it after his execution.
He wants to eat it in the morning. One guard thinks about
Heaven's Gate when she hears the request. Didn't Kool-Aid
have something to do with that choice, with all those people
who died in their matching sneakers? She can't remember if
the Kool-Aid existed, and if it did, if it was grape or cherry.
She goes home to check her cabinets. She is hungry for cherry,
cherry anything. She is pulling the wallpaper off. The bare
wall behind it like a bad commandment. Victor Ferguer, a
drifter, arrived in Iowa in the summer of 1960 and phoned
doctors alphabetically in a phone book claiming he needed
medicine for a woman in trouble. One doctor came to his aid
and Ferguer kidnapped and murdered the doctor. He was the
last man to be hanged in Iowa. What did he request for his last
meal? A single olive. Or, more precisely: "A simple olive with
the pit still inside." After his death, police found the pit in his
pocket. The hard whisper of a tongue.

>>>>

For a while, your lover is a sound guy who works at a local amphitheater. He can walk into any room and tell you where the sweet spot is. It is a nervous habit, this finding; he does it by snapping twice. He takes you to the apartment he shares with friends in the town where Lucille Ball was born. His room is simply a tall curtain drawn across the space. Before you fuck for the first time, he asks if you are ready. He doesn't say this seductively—he is being careful, and does in fact want an answer. Perhaps this is how to love queerly; you say *yes*, not knowing how to define what the yes is for. It is a moment you will never quite forget—he was asking something ineffable, and somehow, you were able to reply: *yes*.

>>>>

You purposely don't watch movies with the word "Miracle" in the title. Even the popular movie with the little girl who grew up in real life and drowned. People still talk about the mysterious circumstances of her death, about how she was in a movie where the other leads died tragically—a car crash in '55, a stabbing in '76. All these people once famous, now all but forgotten. That's how it goes. No miracles. You watch old black-and-white movies with your roommate for an entire month. Eventually, during every movie, your roommate says, *Isn't it weird that all of these people are dead?* When discussing the 1944 film "Meet Me In St. Louis," no one ever really talks about Tootie, the youngest of the family's five children. Tootie seems to be cast as merely adorable, sneaky, emotional in a way understandable to a being who is five or six. But Tootie has a wild darkness. She talks about burying her dolls in a cemetery. *She has four fatal diseases*, Tootie says of one doll, *but all you need is one.* She sings a song about drunkenness to a teenage crowd of partygoers, then later on Halloween tells the maid that she is dressed as "a horrible drunken ghost"; *I died of a broken heart*, she says, *I've never even been buried because everyone's scared to come near me.* Toward the end of the film, when the family is supposed to be moving the next day, she runs out of the house crying and destroys the snow people which the family has built, with a surprising degree of violence: *Nobody's going to have them, not if we can't take them to New York!* she shrieks, stabbing a long black umbrella into the heads and bodies of the snow people, *I'd rather kill them if we can't take them with us!*

>>>>

A man asks his lover to kiss his eyelids. He kisses them, one after the other, just once. They are not in bed together, just sitting side by side drinking coffee. It is a gesture that his lover will remember, and use as a measure against all other intimacies.

>>>>

When I was young I had bibles thrown at me because I was gay,
says a friend. You imagine she means this literally. This child
watching the paper-thin sheaves in their leather-bound frame
flying through the air, as if to immolate her. The new casino
slumps in the river beside the highway. You are stuck in traffic
on the west side; the ball game is just letting out, fans like a
stream of beetles in black and gold. From the backseat, your
kid is asking about the river. She wants to know why you never
swim in the river, why "you and nobody ever" swims there.
It's polluted, you tell her. *The whole river is polluted? Yes the whole
river. But water moves in a river right? Yes water moves. But what
comes off the land is pollution and the river carries that.* Your kid is
quiet. She is looking at the river. *So the water is okay when it gets
here, but when it leaves, it's not? Something like that,* you tell her.
Something like that.

>>>>

Craig shovels the sidewalks of his neighbors without asking them if they want it, salts the driveways cleared of snow. After, he sits at the window in his living room pretending not to watch, waiting for them to come home, angled on the couch so that over the top of his book he can see the street. This is too simple to be fiction. It is just the story of your lonely friend on New Year's Day. You are speaking on the phone; he is watching the street. *Oh man,* Craig says, *George just got home... he's walking up the steps now, he's looking around, like, "Oh wow. Who did this?"* There is some tendon made between him saying this and you listening: something involuntary, sore. You still are surprised when you see your name typed on prescription bottles. There's a part of you that feels special for having your name typed on a sticker and there's another part of you that sees it and feels dread. They are like little marquees for what is wrong with you. Still, seeing it is like someone saying your name out loud after not hearing it for a long time. You're grateful. You line the bottles up a certain way in your cabinet. In a neat row. Each one with your name facing out. You've spent your life learning the different dialects of grief. You master how to speak one. Then another. Then another. Another.

>>>>

Today, you took someone's face into your hands, because she was weeping, holding a rose plucked from one of the many rosebushes outside of a church you'd walked by together. You don't remember exactly the last time you took someone's face into your hands without thinking about it—it was just what the universe seemed to do at that moment, almost without either of you entirely. You stood on the dusty street together like that for a moment, surprised, exact. The feral cats in the yard don't need you, but you feed them anyway. You feed them so that the little peach one will come close enough for you to see its steady-colored eyes. These cats are the color of the street's dust but warmer, a color close to the inside of a conch shell. A place something lived once.

>>>>

At Luna Park, attractions such as the "Infant Incubator" dazzled visitors. A 1906 brochure for the park advertised, "Little mites of humanity, whose lives were despaired of, were taken to the incubator, where, under the care of learned physicians, and the mild ministrations of trained nurses, the park patrons saw them grow strong and sturdy again." You told me about the clock factory that women worked at during World War I, where they were encouraged to drink uranium to make their cheeks rosy. That's what their bosses said: *Rosy*. You said the women actually glowed in the dark. Imagine women walking out of the factory after their shift like a string of Christmas lights. Imagine them twirling in their summer dresses on a dance floor in front of a bandstand. You told me many of them became horribly disfigured, that in one case, a doctor literally reached into a girl's mouth and took out her jaw; that the uranium bore holes in their bones. Every toothbrush you've ever used in your life still exists somewhere. Think about that. You are living temporarily in the house of a musician friend a little less than an hour from San Francisco. He is working on a new album in the basement, and you can hear little slips of his latest. One song is called "American Canyon." One song has lyrics that go *Help me, Armageddon.*

>>>>

A woman is yelling *Hold your sister's hand!* over and over in the grocery store parking lot and it occurs to you that if you had a sister who died this would be a sad thing to hear. But you don't have a sister who died. You don't even have a sister. A piece of what elegy can do is hold an absence by naming it, as if, by saying its endlessness, it is, for a moment fixed in time, when so often there seems no end to grief, only its opening. Even a poem on endlessness has an ending, a hand, for a moment, resting on one's shoulder. Only after they sell the sailboat do your parents tell you about the time they capsized out on the lake where they summer. Your father at 79, your mother atn 68. What happened is that the boat "turtled," the term for a sailboat flipping fully over, the verticality of the mast inverted. You ask your mother what she said as they were going over and she tells you that she didn't say anything, then guesses that, probably, she said your father's name—*It happened so quickly*, she says.

>>>>

When you learned the word "pansexual," your life began to make more sense. All the boyish girls you fell for, the girlish boys. The late '90s Teen Beat magazine photographs you tore out and taped on the inside of your locker, because everyone else was doing it: those boys whose floppy hair fell into their eyes. You kiss somebody trans and the coyote loping by at dawn seems to stop and smile at you, as if all your life it had offered you a riddle, and finally, you got it. Being pansexual doesn't mean that you are attracted to more people than anyone straight or gay might be. It just means that desire is a kaleidoscope, and you are all of the pieces inside.

>>>>

When you were a kid, you woke up once in the farthest back seat of a school bus, just as it was parking in the huge lot of school buses. Yellow ridges outside the window. Somehow, you had fallen asleep, hadn't gotten off at your stop. No one woke you; it must have been that none of the other kids knew you were there. You woke with terror, the long aisle empty and seeming longer for its emptiness, the driver rustling in the driver's seat done with his day. Is this a memory? Or is it a bad dream you've repeated to yourself so many times over that you believe it to be real. The memory of terror is so palpable, the hard green plastic of the far far-back seat. You text your mom, to see if she remembers this, or if it's just another bad dream you've made for yourself, because you always believe you are the kind of person these things happened to. Who had these things happen to them. Your mom texts you back. She says it happened. She can't remember though now if it was her or your dad who came to get you. So. It was real after all. And now, perhaps, it is worse.

>>>>

Every Friday, I went to therapy in Santa Monica and sat with
the therapist's cat, Vivace. I chose to stay in therapy because
of Vivace. *I wonder what is going to happen next*, the therapist
said. After each session, I went to watch the skateboarders
on Venice Beach, with my empty, empty head. The sunken
pool of the skatepark like the doubled why of hips. Once when
I came out of the studio after a ceramics class, the entire
length of the street was closed. People were standing around
in clusters on the sidewalks even though traffic was blocked
off and the empty street itself was open. Close to the center
of the intersection, there was a single black boot on its side,
and beside the boot, a rash of blood. *The ambulance just left,*
someone murmured to me from a close-by cluster, *a biker guy
died.* I went home and got into the shower, the off-tune ice
cream truck clumsy on the corner as usual. Years later, I can
still see that boot. That rash of blood.

>>>>

In spite of everything, there are still invocations, alignments. We find ourselves accidentally brushing arms, legs, hands. On Halloween, we go to The Don't Care Bar to play pool. I dress as Artemis, feathers pinned in my hair, some still connected in wing shape by thin filaments of bone. You wear a heavy necklace made of fishhooks that swing low across the felt. A stranger leans against the florescent claw game, feeding in quarters, trying over and over for the claw to clutch something.

>>>>

In the TV show, Boy meets Girl at a Drive-in. The movie is a backdrop behind them like a horizon. Your life is a lot like that; you came to watch the movie but instead found yourself watching something just in front of it, something obscuring it, a smaller plot dangled in front of you like someone holding up an earring. Like a piece of fruit threatening to fall from a vine. You measure yourself against friends who died. You see their faces airbrushed with makeup in a casket like a used car that's been cleaned-up to sell again on a dingy lot. One friend was buried in a light-blue casket, robin's-egg blue, as if for a child. Her heart just stopped. You watched the casket lower electronically and thought of a baggage claim, how everyone paces around, no longer passengers, waiting to see if what they've brought with them has made it. All your life you have been mourning, so when it came time, goddamnit, you would be a good mourner.

>>>>

Fragments of what is free on Craigslist this week: 15 plastic
1-gallon milk containers; a bullied tetra; canned corn and
ham; a children's book called "Invention!"; a black umbrella
with an ouroboros of poppies. Briquettes. Bricks. Cardboard
boxes. "Excellent condition with lightbulb included." Vanessa
pulls the mattress into the center of her trailer's living room,
and we grope like that a few days, her camo jacket bundled to
be a pillow. We drive around the back roads drinking, her feet
out the window. She talks and talks. She keeps using the word
empath wrong and I don't correct her. When I was little, I had
a friend with a bunch of fool's gold his dad gave him and we
went around to all the grown-ups at a Fourth of July cookout,
asking if they'd trade it with us for quarters. Everyone played
along.

>>>>

Desire seems to work in pointillism. Painting the still world, the sanded gray wind, the white petals slow wind carried on. A woman advises you to *Live on God's Time*, as if it were possible not to. They find the day is cumulous, but their insides swell stratus, sling cirrus. They know *you* is a synonym for cataclysm. The flickering lamp like an insect fossilized in amber. You, as usual, float. Tonight sticks in the leaves. You hear them scraping it down the road. You watched birds hatch and nest for weeks in a drainpipe outside your window and now that they're gone there's a fever woven in you that you can't decide whether to call patchwork or needlepoint. Your friend who had a stroke has to re-learn how to speak. He calls you on the phone. He says: *days, liver, right,* and *bones.* He says: *good morning* and *good evening.* His mom brought him an old Walkman to listen to in the hospital. What he listens to has nothing to do with anyone else. He might as well be living on another planet. A little astronaut just a few streets away from the suburbs, pressing down another word into the ground like a single flag.

>>>>

It is September 11th, 2002. Last year, your first rapist almost died in the Twin Towers, but for some reason, didn't go to work that day. When you finally got through to him, when the call finally went through, he was in his apartment in Spanish Harlem, eating a plum. You had fallen on a stairwell mid-blackout, your wrist dragged by him. The fishnets cut into your hip pressed by the edge of the stair, little bloody X's over a cosmic bruise. Trauma at the edge of vision is a tone of nightshade. *Isn't it ironic?* you said, without meaning to think about Alanis Morissette, how she played an angel or something in that movie, square jaw and heavy-set eyes. You want to catalogue the patterns things leave on our skin, like music notes that disappear. Sixty-three percent of people die with their eyes closed, congruent with how they lived. Evolution has stopped. The fish are full of plastic, mercury, rainbow-finned as the cut you made to your ribcage that winter, after the third time you were raped. You walked for days with only paper towels and tape holding the wound together, like someone in the field at war. I still have a photograph of my first rapist two summers before he was that: his back, sunburned, the white linen pants he was proud of, an arm reaching into the closet in his studio apartment. The thin window above the sink bricked over. Later, streetlights in two slashes sunk over the mattress where I pushed him away once, then twice, then harder, until he turned towards the wall. *You're too young to be in this bed*, he said. I went out to the fire escape. I looked at the city. Then I went back to bed with him, this boy turned away from me, violence sharpening slowly in him like a knife dragged against a stone. I wouldn't be smart again for years.

>>>>

Out of all the angry white people who break into the Capitol Building one day, weeks before the next presidential inauguration, the most photographed is the bare-chested man wearing a long fur hat with massive horns protruding into the air, his face painted in some version of the American flag. *You're very special*, the president tells him, *I love you, go home.*

>>>>

Mitochondrial. Hail beating against a windshield on a highway. An odd mutation in the narrative. The tragedy of history depends on who is doing the writing. This is a hard lesson history will teach. Depending on who writes the history. Hungover, you are wrecked by the sun. Sun-wrecked. There are wild nasturtiums all over the city. Down the street is the post office from which the Zodiac Killer had supposedly sent his letters to San Francisco newspapers. In one letter, he included a 340-symbol cipher, which was finally cracked last year. In the letter, he spelled paradise with a C: *Life will be an easy one in paradice death*, went the last line. You walk through the neighborhood and wonder about the cipher he invented, if he came up with it while walking these same streets, looking at the same windows of the same houses with their soft curtains and mermaid lawn ornaments. You walk, and walk, and you look for a code.

A boy once really threw pebbles against my window once, like one might in the movies. It could've been the beginning of a love story. But it wasn't that kind of movie.

>>>>

Magnolia wash of sky from a part in the hotel curtains. The horizon like a password you can't remember; the sound of high heels falling to linoleum like little guillotines. You keep a bundle of quips in your back pocket as a way to explain your disease to nonalcoholics, or, as your people call them, *civilians*: "An alcoholic is like someone who has lost their legs: they never grow new ones"; "Once you are a pickle, you can't become a cucumber again." In the meetings, they say a lot of things. They say: *My mind is a bad neighborhood: I don't go there alone; This*, they say, *was the last house on the block.* Your sponsor tells you to get a service position. You stand at the door of the AA clubhouse and open the door for people for one hour, one day a week. Beside the clubhouse is a strip club called Deja Vu. The clubhouse is on the other side of some train tracks. Beyond the train tracks, a two-lane highway. Beyond that, a warehouse, and beyond that, the river.

>>>>

During the Q & A, you ask the famous science journalist if art is still useful in the Anthropocene. You ask anonymously by typing your question into a little box. She is in her living room somewhere. Everyone listening is in a different house. On-screen, you watch her tuck her short hair behind her ears. She says that the problem of aestheticizing the climate crisis is a genuine problem; the nexus between art and action remains unclear; *I can't answer*, she says. In the fall of 1970, a town on the Oregon Coast decides that the best way to dispose of the dead sperm whale is to blow it up. A transportation engineer from the state department organizes a crew to bury dynamite. Townspeople and local news crews crowd the dunes to watch, and as the whale explodes, chunks of rotting flesh rain down, sending the watchers fleeing. One chunk lands on the hood of a car, breaking a windshield. The news reports that no one is hurt. On the 50th anniversary of the event, the town votes to name a park after the whale: Exploding Whale Memorial Park. Your father once brought your older half sister and brother to a beach in Northern California, before you were born, before he met your mother. He lived in steep hills, the kind that folk singers sing about. On the beach, they came across a bird stumbling, covered so thoroughly in oil that it looked like a cormorant but wasn't. Your siblings got upset, wanted to find a towel to wrap the bird in, and take it somewhere to be saved. *The bird will be okay,* your father said, *it just needs the weather to change. The weather will change soon,* he told them.

>>>>

Some nights to calm yourself, you imagine a yellow orb moving slowly around the soles of your feet, your ankles, tibias, fibulas, to your moth-shaped ilium, light moving over the cup of bone there like water gathering. Outside, the leaves are so swollen they're sore. You think of yellow wallpaper, that story about the woman waiting everyone reads in high school, assigned to go home and feel out a moral.

>>>>

The Peters twins, Elijah and Milo, are popular gay pornstars. They accept a call for an interview in Prague: *my brother is my lifeblood, my brother is my boy.* Milo, Elijah. They tell the story of how it began. *We were fifteen. I have never loved anyone else.* The sky tastes like vinegar and deer dreaming. Tumbleweeds grow until they turn away from their roots into the wind, seeds flung out with each turn of air. I purr through the saddle of the mesa. Each spring, the high desert roads a massacre of jackrabbits. The bedspread in Motel Bienvenido has a print of wild horses, roadrunners, railroad tracks. Beside the parking lot, two wings splayed and rusted in the switchgrass—someone's abandoned windchimes. At the edge of town, a motorcycle burns.

>>>>

You catch yourself in the mirror like finding a rupture in a dam. Growing up, your parents had these graphic novels about the Holocaust, where mice were Jews, and Nazis were cats. But there must have been other animals, weren't there? It's never that simple. But you can't remember any of the other animals. You want to be something primordial and/or ancient, like the massive wolves who hunted at the waters-edge, hunting farther and farther and farther offshore, deeper and deeper until one day, they became whales. If you tickle a rat, it will laugh. Scientists studying this removed pieces of their vocal cords, and it was found that the rats who could not laugh were more likely to be bitten by other rats, the ones who were complete with all their parts, who could not tell the difference then between play and aggressive behavior in the rats who could not laugh. And what happened then, to those rats who could not laugh? Perhaps after the experiment, they were put all together into one cage, in their silence. For awhile, your sister was on a medication that made her unable to cry. It wasn't that she didn't want to. She told you how she'd come to the field where a sob lives, but nothing came after, not even the heaviness. It wasn't that she felt nothing— it was simply that the feeling stopped.

>>>>

Early spring in the high desert, deep nights, and half awake you can hear the javelinas gnawing the cactus in the yard. You arrived on Valentine's Day and will leave next month, and because you are only passing through, you let desire run your days. The man with adobe dust in his pockets has a long ponytail the color of dry grass and when he holds your hand to pray in the circle at the end of the AA meeting, you can see his mother, stubbing out Newport Slims in the trailer he grew up in, see the stray dogs she feeds outside the trailer. He has been complaining about the other men at his work site, the meth addicts, their quivering hammers on his last nerve. He tries to hide his laugh on account of his bad teeth, but you always make him laugh. You know that he has to start his car with a long tool instead of a key, and you find this charming. You cannot decide if you are more like the smoke or the dogs of his childhood, and so decide to stay quiet. Instead, you live in this partial thing—the moment of him holding your hand, while you stare at the floor together and pray. While you trudge the road of happy destiny.

>>>>

My father sends an email to me and my siblings. Subject heading: VITAL INFORMATION. He and my mother are going to Chile in a few weeks. The email contains an attached document, which he's titled "Vital Information Upon My Demise." All sorts of things are listed, the things that everyone lists: banks, passports, deeds, birth certificates, executors of the wills. On the list of items in the safe-deposit box, filed under Miscellaneous: "Trick wooden box with a silver dollar in it." I repeat this to myself twice. *Trick wooden box with a silver dollar in it.* I can see myself perfectly, standing in the anonymous bank, on the unknown day, in a black coat in a cold room nearly doubled over, holding this. *Trick wooden box with a silver dollar in it.*

>>>>

Often, you find the moment before touch more erotic than touch itself. After touch, there is only a rush toward an ending of being touched. You think of watching geese taking flight from a man-made lake, how hard their wings must beat before they lift from the water. You see an old video of a little boy turning pages in a book. Each time he opens a page he cups his hands above the book, then makes a motion as if he is gently splashing water onto his face. You cannot recall ever seeing your older sister swim. There are photographs of you together in the bathtub as children. In one, she is wearing a little mask, the plastic snout of a crocodile over her nose. Somehow, you were raised to make your bodies invisible to each other.

>>>>

15 April, 1931: "You know," wrote Virginia Woolf, "I must have a heart—it's the only explanation." A home in the woods. A place by the shore. You learned once that touching a moth harms them, how something vital to their flight could come away on your hands. Your friend tells you about how she walked along the edge of a pond, angry in her third year of cancer. How the pond said, *The world is dense, and intimate, and strange.*

>>>>

A headline, nearly a year into the global pandemic: "Japan Appoints a Minister of Loneliness." You're walking out of the pharmacy thinking about ruined car seats and pointless countdowns, missed appointments with your slew of so-and-sos. Your neighbor catches you crying in the shed where you used to smoke together, beside the dead stove and extension cords and crusted cans of paint. For awhile, you don't wipe away your tears, as if letting them rest on your cheeks could soften him towards you, as if, like a movie, he'd reach over with his sleeve to brush a tear away. But this isn't the movies. It's not even a good story. It is a bright Sunday afternoon in February. *I feel like a dying star,* you tell him.

>>>>

Dawdling down the sunny hill, I could claim I was the picture of innocence, but I'd already learned to lie by then. I was ten, wearing my light-blue softball uniform. The long car that slowly approached as I made it to the curb was driven by a man who called out to me, asking for directions. *Can you see this*, he asked, when I approached the passenger door. I could see: his cock in his hand. For years, I never told anyone. After the climactic scene it is usual to refer to what directly follows as "falling action," though more accurately translated, as "the action of falling." Freytag's ziggurat. This is the space of reversals, of wordplay, bitch slaps, assassinations. This is not to say *I told you so,* but rather, *There is nothing else to say.* Or, *I'm only going to say this once.*

>>>>

The first halfway good poem I ever wrote was about a cat,
trying to call in my cat at dusk when I was a child. *I thought
all love would be like that,* the poem went, *rushing out of the dark
with the sound of a tiny warm bell.* Outside, the breeze is like a
discarded magazine, images no one sees, gossip like apostrophe
after apostrophe. When I take a drive, everything looks like a
collage, all the people and buildings cut and pasted. Daylight
like paper cuts.

>>>>

Sometimes we would carpool to high school. There was a day when we stopped at a red light beside an empty lot except the lot wasn't empty. There were two police cars and an ambulance, driven up on the dirt, yellow police tape that formed a square. In the square was some kind of heavy brown tarp covering the shape of a body. The memory doesn't make sense. Shouldn't there have been more action? More police? Shouldn't we have not been able to see this? The red light was no longer than any light. We looked. We did not speak. The light turned green, and we went to school. Reverend Dr. Martin Luther King Jr. wrote a sermon called "A Knock at Midnight." It is rarely quoted. "It is midnight in the social order," he wrote.

>>>>

Some arborists are cutting down a very tall dead pine and
the neighbor kids are screaming. They are screaming the way
Maria screams over Tony's body in the basketball court at
the end of West Side Story: she demands that Chino give her
the gun; she asks him how the gun works, asks him about the
bullets—*How many can I kill and still have one for me*, she spits.
The neighbor children are screaming hurling-oneself-into-an-
open-grave-over-the-casket screams. There are words with
the screams that you can't quite make out. It is unmistakable:
they are screaming for the tree, on behalf of the tree. They
are screaming something like *Oh my God, Oh my God* over and
over and over again. Their mother is a single mother, a Czech
woman with a dark mole below her left eye. Her children all
have names that sound to you like mythological creatures; they
remind you of The Lost Boys in Peter Pan; most days, they run
past your window like a tunnel of sweet noise. When they run,
it changes the light. You leave things for them on your stoop
as if they were stray cats. Rainbow stickers, embroidery floss.
Sometimes at night, the mother knocks on your door with the
slightly expired food she collects from a parking lot where they
hand out slightly expired food to those who want it. One night,
you open the door and she is holding a massive glass jar of
milk, and she doesn't understand why you politely decline to
take it. But what could you do, alone, with all that milk.

>>>>

You start dating someone nonbinary and your father keeps messing up their pronouns. He is 81, and says that using they/them is confusing. He asks why newly made words can't be used, *Binzo / Binzago*, he suggests. You do believe he is trying his best. Is that enough? You text your parents a picture of the flowers your lover has bought for you, a bouquet of sunflowers. *Them sure do seem to make you happy*, your father texts back. *They*, you reply, *and yes.*

>>>>

Bitter rain hangs on the new cherry buds, freezing overnight. Autocorrect keeps changing "poem" to "palm." *Try me*, the world keeps saying. For two years I kept a yellow Post-it Note on the wall by my desk, with a quote by Edna St. Vincent Millay written in pencil: "There is no shelter in you anywhere." Another post-it note, John Donne: "Those are my best days, when I shake with fear." Holy Sonnet XIX. Someone has a little gold-sprayed plastic god on a chain around their neck. How hungry I was for idols in my childhood, aching over all the altars in the brick and chain-link yards, the fake flowers at the feet of weatherworn plaster Virgin Marys. That whisper of her blue shawl despite the sleet of rust belt winters.

>>>>

A six-pack, a car, and the juniper air. The motel Bible and the
ice machine whirring like a heart monitor. The tattoos I used
to draw on your left breast with a pen—a compass, a bridge.
Another picturesque silence. A can of pop for a quarter, the
smell of dead fish near the pier. At dawn there is a tilting run a
robin takes, a forward unlatching. Let's play that game where
we're still unmarked. For a week, I eat nothing but saltines in
the bleached name you knew me by, in the spine of that name.
Each side as sharp as the other. The television blue. The room
like a sonogram.

>>>>

Your father teaches you to ride a bike by holding a handful of M&M's and running ahead of you far down the long road beside the lake. If you catch him, you can have the M&M's. It sets a precedent. One has to be hungry. How many syllables are there really in "memory"? I believe it depends on how badly you want it. Don't mistake me: I am as afraid of ruining this as I have been of anything. I don't know if I believe anymore that there are best words in their best order. There is only what one leaves behind.

>>>>

I knew a man once who had made a film about seed saving. He looked like a Greek statue. Kissing him made very little sense but it seemed like a compliment, one someone gives who doesn't know you whatsoever. I drove to the hills where he lived and after a single night, he decided he could not love me after all. I drove north along the Pacific Coast Highway. Took a video of the dim ocean in the drizzle. We spoke a few years later. He told me he was making a new film. I don't remember now if it was about smoke or about fire. I judge a person by their pills. Holy basil, fish-oil tablets, biotin. I put a pill made for epileptics on my tongue. It does something else for me. The doctor who gave it to me in San Francisco wore a translucent blouse. The doctor who gave it to me in Detroit had African masks on their walls. The doctor who gave it to me in Orlando had books about psychedelic mushrooms lining the bottom shelf in his office. When is this over?

>>>>

A mysterious steel monolith is found in the middle of the Utah desert, and spills across the news. It is discovered by a helicopter full of public safety workers counting sheep. As quickly as it appeared, it disappears, then appears again, a week later on a plateau near a small town in Romania. On the radio, the mayor says that they feel lucky to have been chosen. *There is no reason to panic for those who believe there is still life in the universe*, he says. Weeks later, another article about the monolith. A person had gone out to take pictures of it one night and discovered a few men dismantling its lengths. Turns out, from the pictures he'd taken of the dismantling, that the interior of the monolith was made of plywood. No sci-fi. No conspiracy. Just people. More and more, you feel, there is no mystery left. *Attention is the doorway to gratitude*, you remind yourself.

>>>>

You get involved with your Eastern Religions professor whose parents were missionaries in Mexico when he was young, and they all used to speak in tongues. He is young to be a professor, but you are younger. He tells you how they crossed borders in the war zone of Tangier, how they moved then on the front winds of Katrina in New Orleans, migrated back east when the waters began to rise. You know he's always lived in places breaking with disaster—he has taken up residence in you. When you wake crying one night, he takes a pad of Post-it Notes and tells you to lie on your stomach. He says that he is writing the things he loves about you on each Post-it. Places the Post-its on your back until your skin is covered. You will not remember ever seeing what he wrote there, if he wrote anything at all. You are both trying to stop drinking. There will be a day when you find him on the street and ask if he is drunk, though you know he is. He will smile at you coldly, and say no. It will be the only smile in your life you'll ever be able to describe as cold. A philosopher with an orange mohawk is explaining Time. He says that Time (in general) is perfect, only humans fuck it up. Heaven's being dismantled as we speak—don't listen to any other story. You try a pill called Sarafem, then one called Zoloft, one called Celexa. You wonder where they get these names. Sunrise continues to click on.

>>>>

My friend calls and says that she wants to kill herself because she didn't get into college. There's nothing I can do besides remind her that the world is full of rejection. The next day, she calls from a Wendy's parking lot—she's on Xanax after an emergency trip to the psychiatrist. Her psychiatrist is a saint. I think of the story about the boy who cried wolf—did the wolf get him in the end or not? My friend is babbling, says she's been waiting on two junior cheeseburgers for so long that by the time they arrive, they'll be seniors, ha-ha. *Ha-ha,* I say. On the radio, a newscast about a shooting in Connecticut, an explanation of how our bodies are made from ancient, exploding stars. The newscaster suggests we are being swallowed by a darkness that is surely coming, chilled and sore, but it is not the darkness we should be afraid of, that which will take us. It is what is most clear, most apparent. It is what blazes with clarity before us: a perfect window. A familiar scene. That's how it'll go.

>>>>

A cougar is rumored to have eaten half a baby goat. When they shoot it in the hills, a rope is found to have been tied around its neck so long the skin grew over, like the crest of a wave. Some pet as a cub, never grown quite wild enough to leave the circumference of town. Think of the sounds it swallowed. The Central Valley's crops flash, narrowing. I kept a fortune from a fortune cookie once in my wallet for many years: *Suppose you can get what you want...* The ellipses were included. There is so much shit you can't make up. Once in the woods near my childhood home, I found a hypodermic needle beside a clutch of daffodils growing from a drift of dead leaves. This sounds like a metaphor, but it isn't. I have never been good with fiction.

>>>>

Why pick the shape of a triangle for two people involved with the same person? Especially when the affair is more of a circle, a shape that devours itself. You bought your kid one of those toys where you have to put the right shapes into the right spots. There they are: trying to put a square into a circle, a triangle into a square. There is no way to explain to them that there are so many spaces where nothing goes. The Smashing Pumpkins are singing "1979" and Julia is sitting with her back to the bed crying. Outside the big window, there is a sailboat race. The judge shoots a gun off to signify something, but you can't remember whether the sound means that it is the beginning or the end. John sends a postcard from Alaska, where he has gone to work on a fishing boat, trying to forget he's in love with you. Having a lover of the same gender is like doing a puzzle that needs no picture, no pattern. It is all color. The only way to do the puzzle is to find the pieces that fit together, to find the right edges. To feel them.

>>>>

A common inertia. A spell. We are human so we are confused.
Everything is an antonym. Yet here we are looking for parallels,
for twins. Why look? Why wait? A half-yellow, half-unbeaten
sunlight is making itself known across the sky. Where the rest
of it is doesn't matter. We can hang, split, from every answer.
We can halve and break away. Erode into mountains; reshape
seas; gather into a pile of stones. We don't need to be whole or
finished. Why would we? Why when we can be so beautifully
estranged. Unescorted, unattended. One great unresolved. My
neighbor tells me that his daughter has a spirit in her bedroom,
and he wants my help with it. I go to the bedroom. It is full
of the pink marshmallows of anime, pink octopus, pink violin.
My neighbor shows me the path where he feels the spirit is—it
goes right up to the closet. When I open the closet, there in
the clutter is a long, flimsy mirror, the kind college kids stick
on their dorm-room doors. Directly above the mirror, on the
threshold of the closet door, my neighbor has painted a sea-
green compass. *There's your problem right there*, I think, like a
plumber.

When otters sleep, they wind a bit of kelp around one foot, to keep them from floating away. One otter will hold the paw of another and another. You learn that this arrangement, the otters holding paws like this, is called *a raft*.

>>>>

Today the headlines are about a woman breathing: she'll be
out of the woods if there are no complications in the next 24
hours. Georgia, our drowsy magnetism, our dawn pitching
forward. Deceit takes poise and desire. I learn a new meaning
of *arm's length*. I drive as if on the rails of light rising from car
dealerships along the side of the interstate home—the erosion
of the soul, as you say, is very real. Your spit blesses my long
drive back east. Breaking news: she's blinking. They say that
she recognizes her husband. Then they say she doesn't know,
they were wrong. What is it, really, to be living. We're fucking
amateurs.

>>>>

Your father calls to plan a surprise party for your mother.
Since your mother is listening, he is lying about the afternoon
of the party. He is so bad at lying he almost sounds like a
child. How sweet it is, you think, listening to your father lie.
You remember in school the art teacher having the class make
pictures using red tissue paper. The idea was to tape or glue
the tissue paper in such a way that it resembled a Pentecostal
flame. She hung pictures all around the art room so all the
kids looked like saints. You were made to walk around school
with your pockets out of your pants to make sure you hadn't
stolen anything. You were always like that. At the bottom of a
stairwell, pockets out. A rite of passage. A body like a fish being
cleaned.

>>>>

All day is various degrees of gray. It's like God ran out of paint.
There are some great pieces of art made entirely with only the
color gray. There are photographers who choose to primarily
take only black-and-white photos. "The Americans" by
Robert Frank, one of the most famous books of photography,
is entirely black and white. Picasso's "Guernica" is gray.
Rothko's "Untitled (Black on Gray)" is gray. "The Gray Tree"
by Piet Mondrian is gray. This was the day I met you. There
was a small window in the bathroom of the apartment where
I was staying that looked out at the harbor. Gray water. Gray
ships passing. Gray sounds—*guise, gauze, graze, ground, gone.*

>>>>

On the jukebox, the Stones are singing "As Tears Go By,"
fifty years of diner smoke troubling the sound. The same
waitress saying *Honey* in a hundred voices. The streetlights are
bleeding. They are an engine inside this spectacle, an economy
of air and friction. I gather myself on the road like a mud-
dried paperback, ruined and unfolding. Taxis hiss by, smooth
yellows. In the alley, police left their lights flashing and woke
me. I counted six cops and two men in handcuffs. A real bird
clutched a real branch and its song made a door in the night.
There was nothing small about it. The men in handcuffs
seemed unhurried, as did the cops. The scene of the men was
noiseless; I was sure, if they knew someone was watching, the
sound would rush back into the scene; I held my breath. I
stood at the window and watched, like a semicolon.

>>>>

"Arborescent," a term coined by the French philosophers Deleuze and Guattari, is basically used to describe "unidirectional progress, with no possible retroactivity." More than simple gallows humor, the dissociative method is a refusal of closure: instead of composing distanced elegies, she writes *into* the dead.

>>>>

Part of what I liked about living in Los Angeles was the store
called the 99 Cent Store. I liked buying single packets of miso
soup and Mexican candy and off-brand mascara. I liked
crossing the parking lot towards the wild pink 99 Cent neon
sign, thinking about cents, the way I did when I was young
and collected coins from foreign places. Everyone seemed to
collect things when I was young—baseball cards or porcelain
horses. Kids don't seem to collect in the same way now. One
late fall I collected ten empty nests. Some of them had plastic
strips woven in to their curve. *Insulation*, joked a friend. It
made me think of those pictures of dead birds on the beaches,
their stomachs cut open, the dozens of types of plastic inside.
Doom confetti.

>>>>

Barrel organ music above the dark miraculous earth. When the Ferris wheel rests at its uppermost height you can see your house and the marsh beyond it. The wheel is close to coming to its last stop for the night this season. *Heave-Ho*; time to move along; caravans following the twenty-four-hour man, his paint pointing to the next town, the next and another town, all those green-yellow-blue-red bulbs that must be strung up in another elsewhere. The carnival smells masked, animal, like grease and dank hay and fried dough, like the smell of quarters boys will spend on the rifle game. From where you are, swaying in the air, for a moment, you can see your life laid out before you. A railing we hung from. A disentanglement. Careful, careful.

>>>>

I was thirteen or so when I learned that girls do, after all, have sex with girls. The book was about a cowgirl—on the cover, she straddled the moon. There had been books delicately placed in my room that explained *What's Happening to My Body?* with garish cartoons, swing-dancing characters wearing striped T-shirts emblazoned with the words ESTROGEN! and TESTOSTERONE!, characters bending in un-human ways to examine their armpits sprouting with brambles, goofy boys pulling their pants horizontal to gawk down with saucer eyes. I moved in my body as if it were an empty Tupperware container. But in the cowgirl book, a girl rode another girl's thumbs. And then, for awhile, I knew something about my body. I used to imagine my dead child all the time. Sometimes people don't think of their abortions as having been children, but I do. It has nothing to do with religion, just with something that clicked inside me, like a whistle only a dog can hear.

>>>>

Someday will come like the gold twang of a singing bowl; a new
cure in an alchemist's beaker; the many blending molecules in
a puddle beside a deserted lot. Twig or blossom, shatter or
fracture; slow dancing on thin air, a paisley scarf floating in
Dolores Park. For now though, there's only the copper dog
gnawing a tennis ball, yet still, I'm expecting someday like a
pardon or a rose silk slip. Still, I'm expecting someday like
warm sun falling across the wooden floor. Because look, there:
warm sun falling across the wooden floor.

>>>>

Strawberry moon. Harvest moon. Buck moon. Blood moon. Worm moon. Blue moon. Wolf moon. Snow moon. Corn moon. Frost moon. The moon is two-spirit. I can't help but anthropomorphize it, as something that takes pity on us. A split seed. I look up at the exact moment clouds have parted for the moon, making the circle of clouds into the color of embers, and think of the names ancient astronomers gave to those deeper grays of the moon, mistaking their color for bodies of water. Sea of Knowledge. Sea of Cold. Sea of the Edge.

>>>>

Autumn came and went. Shut itself inside its box of leaves. Now the first snow. What's to say about it but how quiet it is. How it makes the metal in your teeth ache. How it makes the places where you've hurt yourself deepen like canyons, like mines. It is like how water keeps pouring from a waterfall, you know? You like the myths that have to do with water. The turtle whose back holds the world. A king who rules the sea. A mermaid whose comb in your hair will kill you. The snow of the world is thinning. You go to a documentary with your parents called *Chasing Ice*, about how the glaciers are dying. The theatre is cold and the little boys sitting a few rows ahead won't pay attention, because they don't know any better. You learn that the word for a piece of a glacier breaking from the whole is called "calving." To help an uneasy birth, a farmer will tie chains to the legs of a calf. It is important to pull the calf quickly then—the umbilical cord is breaking; it is important to help the calf be fully born so that it can start breathing; the time has come when it will either begin to breathe, or it will never breathe.

>>>>

The concrete floors of your loft were painted red. When you'd relapse, I'd sit outside the heavy metal door, sliding notes and chocolate bars underneath once a day. Hear you shuffling on the other side. Eventually, when you'd open the door, the air would reek of cool mint and vomit. No liquor stores are open in Pennsylvania on Sundays; empty plastic bottles of Listerine were piled in the sink, the kind with at least eight fluid ounces. You sat on your bed, and I put on your socks. Tied your shoes. We had a game we always played when we sat in the intake room of the hospital—they won't allow anyone in until their blood alcohol level drops to a certain point. So we came up with a game to pass the time, to make one another laugh. You were dead drunk but I suppose you knew I needed it, or maybe I started the game, I don't know how it started, how many times we sat in that room, the numb television bolted to the wall. Your personal items taken by the nurse, put in plastic. I'd name a thing, and you'd tell me what the trouble with that thing was. Lizards, bagels, ChapStick, pencils. Once during the game, I offered the ponies of Chincoteague, the ones that swim together each year from one island to another. You couldn't find anything wrong with them.

>>>>

You land in Florida with a terrible fever and lie in your hotel bed with the fever surrounding you. You think: frozen vineyard; Ernest Shackleton. Another thing biological men never wonder about is when they will bleed next. This perhaps is the sharpest difference among genders.

>>>>

There are businesses that will turn your ashes into vinyl records. There are businesses that will turn your ashes into diamonds. There are businesses that will shoot your ashes into space. When I die, I want to be buried. That, or I want my ashes to stay only ash. I want to burn the fire back.

>>>>>

Narcissus tattooed backward on his chest. The belt that broke the time he tried to hang himself. His punctured lung. How his father broke his collarbone in a fight, and it healed wrong. It is always winter when you think of him. His always crisp white shirts, shined shoes, his collar upturned against the winter. There is a game of hide-and-seek you play with the horse on the wall, the shadow you've made a horse who leaves with the moon. You have started to name the pieces out loud—cold light of day shaped like nothing-like-day. Do not assume to tell me what I have or have not looked away from.

>>>>

Your worst scar is along your ribs, a scar that you cut across the right side, though you are left-handed, and perhaps that's why you cut it, as if the hand that held the blade was less yours. You used to have names for this scar, excuses: *The Worm King; I was attacked by a tiger.* There are people who have the job of putting broken things together. People who only use broken things to fix other broken things. To them, any old junkyard is heaven. All they need are some bolts; some screws. Duct tape. Time. Just sunshine, moving through the house like an old woman who refuses to leave a home she can no longer live in alone. You can tell a lot about people by pictures they take of themselves. Sometimes, all day, you look at pictures people take of themselves. A perpetual news cycle of self-portrait. One woman takes a picture of herself crying every day. There is a reason she is doing it, she says in the caption. Here is a picture of her crying. And here is another. Like I said, there is one for every day.

>>>>

In your younger brother's favorite video game, the protagonist is a blue hedgehog. The point of the game is to run as fast as you can. The end is endlessly grinding away. *Hurry!* says the screen. You've been seeing more erasures lately. People cutting away and erasing words and using what's left to express something. A newspaper. A textbook. A bible. Erasure is the art form of our times.

>>>>

For four years in a row, each day of spring and summer, a turtle appears at a lady's back door, and each day, she gives it a pancake. Then one day, she catches a glimpse of the turtle on the grass beside the street, and sees a man stop his car. He picks up the turtle and drives away with it. Upon threat of separation, captive pairs of swans have been known to asphyxiate themselves with almost simultaneous accuracy. I confess that I wish I believed in God, and you say *Just then, I was praying for you.* You are whispering a story of crossing a rope bridge in the dark. In the story, it is not important whether you make it across.

>>>>

You keep having the hope that this is a prologue but no one knows how far they are into their own story. Some of us are hoping it's the end.

>>>>

My first cousin who died, who I barely knew, gave me the pink
bear I slept with every night as a child. She died alone in her
apartment and no one knew for a few days. The bear came
with a single thread sewn across her mouth of a single thread,
fixed in a smile. At some point, long before my cousin died, I'd
had my mother clip the thread that held my bear's mouth. I
wanted the bear to be able to show herself. To show if she was
happy or sad. Or whatever. We are having a fight. Over what?
You are chopping potatoes with your back turned to me, and
when you turn you are holding both a potato and the knife. I
know you will throw one or the other and I duck.

>>>>

You cannot help but convince yourself you have cancer. A toothache. A numbness. A dull pain in your shoulder. All cancer. On TV, soldiers are in a cemetery shooting rifles. They are totally silent. Then there's a gunshot. Then there's another. Then: silence. America.

>>>>

You drive across the country with your fiancé for a month and a day, camping nowhere for more than a single night, a dog-eared atlas tucked beside the passenger seat, your routes highlighted with a yellow highlighter you keep in the glove compartment. He isn't used to driving, and so you drive whenever the weather is risky. When you reach San Francisco, you stay with a friend for one night, then two, and something about stopping sours the space between you. You sit alone on a roof in the Castro, watching the foggy morning slip over bright houses on the hillside. You walk in a cool room amongst minerals. The mineral hall is full of mirrors. Your parents used to leave you in the museum sometimes as if it were a babysitter, giving you a time to meet them at the tremendous ageless doors. You memorized the dioramas, the leopard tearing into the flesh of an iguana. The couplet of elk which, if you squinted hard enough, you could believe were moving.

>>>>

You have our unmailed letters. You have your addresses of
the dead. You have a view, a contagion. You imagine a body
bare and undazed, look at your empty hands. The days peel
out like copies. Copies of copies. A carpenter bee works all
summer inside the corner window and we sleep to her jaw's
music. The cat curves to be her own bed—easy to forget we
always have a place to sleep in our hands. Sirens far off and
farther, the poisoned bay. Tomorrow I'll walk along the shore
photographing what has washed up: a collection of bloated
lemons, ashen catfish, bottle caps, a hazard of fishing lines like
knotted veins. Now try and measure that life

>>>>

There is a short period of time after crying that is not crying but like crying. As far as I know, there is no name for that. That moment when the body, exhausted, settles itself. And I'm not going to name it. Are you?

No. I'm not going to name it.

>>>>

I like the Robert Frost poem that begins: *Back out of all this now too much for us.* Once upon a time, there were no drive-bys, no push button massacres. A different type of hardening was required: you carried someone's blood home with you. You had to wash your hands of them. I sit beside my oldest friend, our hands smoothing the last breaths from her dog, after the injection. *Dreamland,* my friend says. The tumor in her dog's heart has grown so large it interrupts his breath. We see in the X-ray the black mass where only long white ridges should be—snow streaking a faraway mountain. My friend on her belly, her mouth at his eye. *I needed you,* she says to him. It is not my moment, so I go stand in the hallway, looking through the window in the door while she sings in the last moments to her dog dying, imagining when next I will be here. Probably, we will do this for one another, when our parents go. The vet stands beside me in the hallway, explaining the shot. *Dogs don't understand euphoria,* says the vet. *He will try to fight it,* she says. What makes the dream terrible is how easy it is to believe.

>>>>

You are going through the notes on your phone. On one page, you have written two things without attribution. A quote, a fact. *Attention is the doorway to gratitude. Fire creates its own wind.* Technology is already erasing our sense of place. Our phones do not know to tell us to turn left at the grove of alders near the long white temple. Instead, they tell us to turn at the Taco Bell. Corporations can pay to be placed on maps, to be landmarks. Turn left at the third McDonald's; exit after Texaco. It's so easy to forget how much of America now is uninhabited by top predators, how so much of what used to be wild here was killed years ago. You soothe yourself with an old routine: you close your eyes and imagine this land as it was before man. The bottom of a prehistoric ocean. All the beasts swimming in the what's-now sky above your head, taking their time, living their lives.

>>>>

I know that the longer I smoke cigarettes, the more lines will appear at the sides of my mouth like parentheses. You text to tell me you've written something so incredibly sad. *You'll love it*, you say.

>>>>

It is obvious that every relationship ends for a different reason. But those reasons are really the same reason: one person changes; one person stays the same. Outside the church after the AA meeting, a nice-seeming lady gives you two laminated bookmarks. On the pink bookmark is a list of "I am" statements. *I am the total of everyone who has ever touched me*, reads one. *I do not fit into what I see*, says another. *I am not ashamed!* says the final statement. There was a chasm, a cheap exaggeration, a mouth like a first aid kit. You know exactly how you'd spend the last day of your life. What you're looking for is some autonomy. Less staccato. Every few minutes, there is another new reason you feel strange. You want to believe that one day, you could be the type of person who sits on a bench and looks out at the sea and only sees the sea. What would that be like? To see only one thing at a time.

>>>>

For miles, there is only one billboard — *Don't drive faster than your guardian angel can fly* – paid for by someone who must have lost someone. *History has its jokes*, the radio preacher laughs. He believes homosexuals have brought these times upon the world. *That's where they live*, says the preacher, *California, New York City, the fallen places which God has decreed the oceans to swallow.* Mercy still lives in America, from what I can see. The story's start is cloaked; mile markers are lit up like eyes of spiders masquerading as dew on a bare branch.

>>>>

Your friend's sister just died and he quit school. He is staying at a place by a lake in Upstate New York. *It's weird,* he says, *I never see any boats.* He looks at the water. The water looks back at him. *What am I going to do with all this stuff?* When you wake each morning, the first thing you think of is your body. You stand naked on the glass scale and see where you are. Your little sister starts talking about what it means to lose weight. *It isn't really lost,* she says, *because when you lose a thing, you can find it again. A lost thing means a whole thing that stays a thing you can hold, right?* You want to tell her about the colloquialisms: losing one's mind, for example, but you don't. Instead, you tell her that she is right. That losing weight should be called something more like shedding weight. She understands this because she likes snakes, cicadas. *So it's a whole thing that disintegrates, and goes back into the earth?* You tell her yes, that it's something closer to that. Something more along those lines.

>>>>

You meet someone on the internet and correspond for a month or two before you decide to meet up. You buy a bus ticket to Tallahassee. They have long blue eyes, creases along the sides of their mouth that remind you of a bloodhound. Your hours together are short—they hadn't mentioned in their letters that they have lupus. You clean their attic apartment while they sleep. They sleep and you watch a reality TV show alone without the volume. The show is about loggers, maybe in Montana, you guess. Many shots of bright chains dragged across the snow. They bring a horse to a funeral. It leans its neck along the casket. *There are in our existence spots of time...,* writes Wordsworth. He means the beginning of something, a kind of structural moment one returns to inhabit, a well of understanding, kairotic time. But it is also the end of something. An absolute moment. A lesson: if a swallow is trapped in one's bedroom, what to do is to turn all the lights out and open a window. The swallow will fly toward the only square of light left. The opened window. What now?

>>>>

It is the two-year anniversary of when your friend's husband killed himself in their shed. He left her a note on the kitchen table, telling her not to look in the shed, and she didn't. A month after his death, she sent you homemade candy. For two years, you have been looking for the right synonym for "strong," as a way to pay respect to her solidity. You haven't found it. She gives their white poodle to her mother and adopts a pit bull mix. A mutt she names Arrow. You wake up hungover again. There is a glass of red wine on the sill. There is a tiny translucent spider drowned in the wine, and you drink it anyway. You've forgotten every word synonymous with remorse, regret. You're unpunctuated. Unnumbered. Alight. The break is not clean, but easy.

>>>>

I give up on the idea of having a child. When asked why, sometimes I mention my finances first. As a shield. Other times, I explain my lack of a partner. It takes so long to know someone. I know myself well enough to know I would be not simply a good parent, but an excellent one, one with a way of moving through the world with the child as burdenless. But I have given up the idea of having a child. How could I bear bringing them into the world? How could I bear the knowledge that I would, someday, leave them, here, to *this*?

>>>>

You stay up late one night reading about pangolins, about how they are the most trafficked animal. You learn that they have no teeth. You interrupt a small collection of ants, carrying a green inchworm. You interrupt them because you think the ants are attacking the inchworm, brushing the ants away with the soft point on a fallen leaf. The ants scuttle away, and when they do, you realize that the inchworm is already dead. *Drink and be whole again beyond confusion*, ends the poem.

>>>>

Two nights at a casino on the border of Utah and Nevada.
The rooms are cheap and surprisingly nice, a triptych of
orchids above the bed. I go down to the windowless lobby
and buy saltwater taffy from the gift shop, spend hours at the
slot machines. Ancient Wheel Bison II. Betti the Yetti. Crazy
Joker. Desert Dawn. Desert Dusk. Eagle Bucks. Fast Hit.
Five Star. Great Tiger. Griffin's Throne. Hoot Loot. Icarus
Journey. Johnny Cash. King Cat. Lady of the Dead. More
Chili. Neptune King. Open Vault. Peacock. Pompeii. Quick
Velvet. Rumble Rumble. Solar Disc. Triple Cash. Underdog.
Vibrant 75. Wild Rose. Wild Wins. XTasy. Zeus. Zenith. *If you
want a happy ending*, said Orson Wells, *that depends, of course, on
where you stop your story.*

>>>>

A donkey named Stella is born without eyes and almost dies as a baby because she cannot see to nurse. When she is two years old, some volunteers at the farm sanctuary think of playing music for her. They bring a boombox to the stable, turn on a religious station. A choir sings in Latin. In Egypt, scientists put a mummy in a sarcophagus inside an MRI machine. They've found a way to recreate the mummy's vocal cords inside a computer. Your son shows you a video of the voice. It is literally just a grunt. *Aaaaggghhh,* the mummy says. You and your son play the sound over and over, laughing. *Aaaaggghhh!* Inside the sarcophagus, a 3,000-year-old inscription which announces the mummy's desire to someday speak again. You tell your son you could never afford to be inside an MRI machine. Stella sways her head from side to side, her broad furry ears smoothly sweeping the air, moving not with the music but inarguably because of it. She stands fixed in one place and the volunteers weep watching her. She listens, swaying, until the song is over.

Note on Creation

This book was written collaboratively over the course of eight months during the Coronavirus pandemic (November 2020– August 2021), in a single shared Word document, from six states away.

A few casual and incomplete Notes, in no order, on References

- The child and its imaginary friend are Calvin and Hobbes, created by Bill Watterson.
- The book mentioned in which Nazis are depicted as cats and the Jewish population is depicted as mice is actually graphic novels titled *Maus* by Art Spiegelman.
- The Robert Frost poem referred to is "Directive" - quotes from this poem are also scattered throughout.
- "Remorse—is Memory—Awake" by Emily Dickinson is the first line of poem 744.
- Martin Luther King Jr. wrote his sermon "A Knock at Midnight" for the Youth Sunday Services of the Woman's Convention Auxiliary, National Baptist Convention, in 1958.
- Freytag's ziggurat refers to the German novelist and playwright Gustav Freytag's theory of dramatic structure, a five-part model commonly referred to as Freytag's pyramid, originally derived from analysis of ancient Greek and Shakespearean drama.
- "Everyday objects shriek aloud" - René Magritte, "La Ligne de vie" (1938), reprinted in *René Magritte*, 1898 – 1967, ed. Gisèle Ollinger-Zinque and Frederik Leen (Ghent: Ludion, 2005), 46.
- "like poetry, whistling does not need to be useful in order to be special and beautiful": this quote is from Antonio Márquez Navarro, speaking to a *New York Times* reporter about a traditional whistling language, called Silbo Gomero, on La Gomera, one of the Canary Islands.
- The line about "how spaces can love and hurt one another as if they were solid" is paraphrased from the book of essays "Many Circles" by Albert Goldbarth.

- The girl who wears a skeleton costume is the singer-songwriter Phoebe Bridgers.
- Cass McCombs is the singer-songwriter of "American Canyon Sutra," and the lyrics "Help me, Armageddon" are from his song "Sleeping Volcanoes."
- "There are in our existence spots of time," appears in William Wordsworth's poem *The Prelude* (Book XII "Imagination and Taste, How Impaired and Restored").
- "Tonight sticks in the leaves" is a line from Frank Stanford's epic poem "The Battlefield Where The Moon Says I Love You."
- "You dance and you shake the hurt" and "All the love in the world can't be gone/all the need to be loved can't be wrong" are lyrics from the song "Boogie Wonderland" by Earth, Wind & Fire.
- The story about a boy whose jaw is broken by his father takes inspiration from the album *Homemade Braces* by the band Secret Tombs, which may be found on Bandcamp.
- "I wouldn't be smart again for years" is the last line of Jim Daniels' poem "March 12, 1982."

Acknowledgments

We are grateful to the readers and editors of *The Adroit Journal*, *The Cincinnati Review*, *Iterant*, *Iron Horse Literary Review*, *The Momentist*, *The Offing*, *Obliterat*, *Puerto del Sol*, *Salamander*, *Salt Hill*, *Tupelo Quarterly*, and *Waxwing* in which excerpts of this book appeared in one form or another.

Gratitudes

We are grateful to the University of Alabama Press and the members of Fiction Collective 2 for believing in us, particularly Marream Krollos for selecting this work as the winner of the 2022 Ronald Sukenick Innovative Fiction Contest.

Sophie would like to express gratitude to Craig Bernier, Gregory Barnett, and Casey Whittier; gratitude to Stacy Dawson Stearns, Ajani Brannum, and all those who experienced and illuminated HUT—thanks for keeping me afloat during the deepest season of Covid isolation. Gratitude to Mandy Monroe and The Bog as a whole. Gratitude to those in The Rooms. Depthless gratitude to her blood relatives, without whom this book would not exist.

Corey would like to express his love and gratitude to Rajani Adhikary for her love, support, and incredible patience during the writing of this book. Thanks to his parents Dean and Susan Zeller. Thanks to his son Malcolm Zeller. Thanks to his oldest and closest friends Jason Arndt, Hank Barbour, Rick Sadlier and Dani Payer. Thanks to his Syracuse family Christopher Kennedy, Victor Hernandez (hermano and bandito), Matthew Winning, Shannon Fabiani, Kellan Head, Aykut Ozturk, and Greg Sevik. Finally, thanks to Rama and Rita Adhikary for their amazing generosity, kindness, and support.